THE
BOO
BELONG
TO

Name: Age:

Favourite player:

2023/24

My Predictions   Actual

Boro's final position:

Boro's top scorer:

Championship winners:

Championship top scorer:

FA Cup winners:

EFL Cup winners:

Contributors: Andy Greeves, Will Miller, Peter Rogers.

A TWOCAN PUBLICATION

©2023. Published by twocan under licence from Middlesbrough Football Club.

Every effort has been made to ensure the accuracy of information within this publication but the publishers cannot be held responsible for any errors or omissions. Views expressed are those of the authors and do not necessarily represent those of the publishers or the football club. All rights reserved.

978-1-915571-55-7

£10

PICTURE CREDITS: Action Images, Alamy, Middlesbrough FC and Press Association

CONTENTS

THE CHAMPIONSHIP
SQUAD
2023/24

Seny Dieng
1

POSITION: Goalkeeper **COUNTRY:** Senegal **DOB:** 23/11/1994

The Swiss-born sweeper-keeper joined Boro in the summer from Queens Park Rangers and quickly slotted in. He played in Switzerland and Germany before joining Rangers and after a string of loan outings he made his first-team breakthrough in 2020. His league debut was in a 1-1 draw with Boro!

An international, he played twice in the 2021 African Cup of Nations as Senegal won the tournament.

Tommy Smith
2

POSITION: Defender **COUNTRY:** England **DOB:** 14/04/1992

After cutting his teeth in non-league football, the tough-tackling right-back was snapped up by Huddersfield and became a fixture. He was captain as the Terriers won at Wembley in the 2017 Play-Off final to reach the Premier League. He then had three successful seasons at Stoke before signing for Boro and his rock-solid displays last term earned him a new deal.

Rav
Van Den Berg

3

POSITION: Defender   **COUNTRY:** Netherlands   **DOB:** 07/07/2004

Boro fought off Euro giants Roma, Bayern Munich and AC Milan to sign the hot prospect Dutch defender from PEC Zwolle in the summer. Rav, who has played for Holland at every level from Under-15 to Under-20, can operate anywhere along the back line. He made his Dutch top-flight debut aged just 16. His older brother Sepp is at Liverpool.

Daniel
Barlaser

4

POSITION: Midfielder **COUNTRY:** England **DOB:** 18/01/1997

The Geordie playmaker started at Newcastle before signing for Rotherham in 2020 after an impressive loan. With his sharp passing he was a key figure as the Millers reached the Championship and lifted the EFL Trophy in 2021. He joined Boro in January 2023 and has added nicely to the midfield mix. He played for Turkey before switching to England at Under-18 level.

SQUAD
2023/24

Dael
Fry
6

POSITION: **Defender**   COUNTRY: **England**   DOB: **30/08/1997**

The Berwick Hills battler is a fixture in the Boro back line and has played over 200 games since his debut in August 2015 aged just 17. Strong, brave and tough in the tackle, Dael signed a new three-year deal in the summer. With England he has won the 2014 Under-17 Euros, the 2017 Under-20 World Cup and the 2018 Under-21 Toulon Tournament.

Matt
Clarke
5

POSITION: **Defender**   COUNTRY: **England**   DOB: **22/09/1996**

The left-sided defender is eager to make up for lost time after an injury-hit first season at Boro. He impressed in his first six games, but suffered a serious back injury and missed the rest of the campaign. Matt started at Ipswich and has clocked up 300 games and won Player of the Year awards at Portsmouth, Derby and West Bromwich Albion.

SQUAD
2023/24

Hayden **Hackney** 7

POSITION: **Midfielder**   COUNTRY: **Scotland**   DOB: **26/06/2002**

Hayden exploded onto the scene last season as Boro's big breakthrough act. Promoted to the first team, the Redcar-born box-to-boxer seized the moment and forged a dynamic engine room unit with Jonny Howson as Boro powered up the table. Last season's Young Player of the Year, he made his England U21 debut in a 3-0 UEFA European Under-21 Championship qualification victory away to Luxembourg in September.

Riley **McGree** 8

POSITION: **Midfielder**   COUNTRY: **Australia**   DOB: **02/11/1998**

The Aussie World Cup star emerged as one of Boro's most potent and entertaining outlets last season as he grew into Michael Carrick's fluid, attacking approach with his intelligent movement and quick feet. Left-sided midfielder Riley started in Australia, but also had spells with Club Brugge in Belgium, Charlotte in the US and at Birmingham before joining Boro in January 2022.

Emmanuel
Latte Lath

9

POSITION: **Forward**   COUNTRY: **Ivory Coast**   DOB: **01/01/1999**

With pace and an instinct for space in the box, the two-footed Ivorian hitman aims to fire the bullets for Boro. Emmanuel joined Atalanta aged 16 and notched his first senior goal against Juventus in the Coppa Italia a year later. After loans in Italy's lower leagues, last year he hit 16 in 34 in the Swiss top flight with St Gallen.

Morgan
Rogers

10

POSITION: Forward   **COUNTRY:** England   **DOB:** 26/07/2002

A skilful and powerful dribbler with quick feet and a fierce shot, Morgan can play anywhere along the front line. He started at West Brom, but was snapped up by Manchester City after impressing against them in the FA Youth Cup semi-final. He had successful loan spells at Lincoln, then Championship clubs Bournemouth and Blackpool before joining Boro in the summer.

Isaiah Jones 11

POSITION: Defender/midfielder **COUNTRY:** England **DOB:** 26/06/1999

Electric Isaiah emerged in 2021/22, his mazy dribbles up the right earning press plaudits, the Young Player of the Year gong and his own terrace chant. The livewire wideman, who joined Boro from non-league Tooting & Mitcham in the summer of 2019, was also awarded the Championship Player of the Month award in December 2021.

Alex Gilbert 14

POSITION: Forward **COUNTRY:** Republic of Ireland **DOB:** 28/12/2001

Alex started in West Brom's Academy, but was head-hunted by Brentford in 2020 after they spotted his quick feet and movement. He captained the Bees' B Team to Premier League Cup victory before following in the footsteps of teammate Marcus Forss by transferring to Boro in search of pitch time. He is a Republic of Ireland Under-21 international.

SQUAD

2023/24

Anfernee Dijksteel — 15

POSITION: Defender   **COUNTRY:** Suriname   **DOB:** 27/10/1996

Amsterdam-born Anfernee arrived as Player of the Year when he joined Boro from Charlton for £2m August 2019. A tigerish right-back, he has great control and passing from his days in the midfield engine room and is quick to join attacks. He made his international debut for Suriname in March 2023.

Jonny Howson — 16

POSITION: Midfield   **COUNTRY:** England   **DOB:** 21/05/1988

Boro's Rolls Royce midfield man continues to dominate games and dictate the tempo and direction of play without ever looking flustered. The former Leeds and Norwich captain has clocked up over 700 senior games now and after six years at Boro the hugely influential skipper leads by example on and off the pitch. A superb partner for Hayden Hackney.

Paddy
McNair
17

POSITION: Defender/Midfielder **COUNTRY:** Northern Ireland **DOB:** 26/04/1995

Versatile Paddy has played in every position in defence, as a right-wing back and in several slots in midfield in his five years at Boro which has made him very useful in a variety of formations for a string of managers. The former Manchester United and Sunderland man is a regular with the Northern Ireland international set-up.

Sammy
Silvera
18

POSITION: Midfielder/Winger **COUNTRY:** Australia **DOB:** 25/10/2000

Mercurial Sammy signed in the summer and quickly caught the eye with flashing feet and jinking runs in his early outings and scored on his first Boro start, in the 3-2 Carabao Cup win at Huddersfield. The London-born winger grew up in Australia and played for Western Sydney, Central Coast Mariners and Newcastle Jets. He is a Socceroo international too.

Josh
Coburn
19

POSITION: Forward **COUNTRY:** England **DOB:** 06/12/2002

Hot prospect predator Josh burst into the spotlight two years ago as he plundered four league goals on cameos from the bench and cracked in a memorable last-gasp FA Cup wonder winner against Spurs. Last term he honed his instinctive skills and beefed up away on loan at League One Bristol Rovers where he got ten goals in 35 league games.

SQUAD

2023/24

Marcus Forss — 21

POSITION: **Forward** COUNTRY: **Finland** DOB: **18/06/1999**

Good feet, intelligent movement on and off the ball and a blistering turn of pace made Marcus a key ingredient in Boro's attacking style under Michael Carrick last season and after settling into a wide right role he scored a useful ten goals in 43 games. The industrious international arrived from Brentford in July 2022. His grandfather also played for Finland.

Hayden Coulson — 22

POSITION: **Defender** COUNTRY: **England** DOB: **17/06/1998**

Gateshead-born wing-back Hayden made a dramatic impression with marauding runs up the left when he broke into the team. He played 29 games in 2019/20, and has had five loan spells since then. A solid shift in Scotland with Aberdeen last season and a strong pre-season earned him a new deal at Boro and he started this term in the team.

Tom Glover

23

POSITION: Goalkeeper   **COUNTRY:** Australia   **DOB:** 24/12/1997

Towering keeper Tom arrived in July 2023 from Melbourne City as a promising 'keeper to boost Boro's Socceroo contingent. He played 98 games for Melbourne over three Premiership title-winning campaigns and also featured for Australia's Under 23s in the 2021 Tokyo Olympics.

Alex Bangura

24

POSITION: Defender   **COUNTRY:** Sierra Leone   **DOB:** 13/07/1999

The attacking left-back started at Dutch giants Feyenoord then moved to Cambuur where he played over 100 games and became captain. He is fast and physical and has also played as a winger so has the ability and instinct to get forward and join the attacks. He joined Boro just before deadline day to compete with Lukas Engel and Hayden Coulson for that spot.

Matt
Crooks

25

POSITION: Midfielder/Forward   **COUNTRY:** England   **DOB:** 20/01/1994

The big-hearted battler has proved versatile playing in midfield, as a No.10 and as the big man up top as Boro chase a game. That has been successful with 'the Tree' developing a profitable taste for late goals, including the FA Cup leveller at Old Trafford as Boro beat Manchester United on penalties. He played for ten clubs before joining from Rotherham in July 2021.

Darragh
Lenihan

26

POSITION: Defender   **COUNTRY:** Republic of Ireland   **DOB:** 16/03/1994

Tough-tackling, good in the air with great positional awareness and an ability to carry the ball out, the experienced centre-back has been a great addition to the Boro back line and has brought the best out of Dael Fry. The Republic of Ireland international joined on a free in June 2022 after 250 games at Blackburn where he was the skipper.

Lukas Engel **27**

POSITION: Defender/Midfielder **COUNTRY:** Denmark **DOB:** 14/12/1998

Having started as a left winger with an eye for goal, summer signing Lukas has the instinct to get down the line and into the dangerzone. He hit 29 goals in 48 games at local club Kastrup, kept it up at Superliga side Vieje then moved to Silkeborg. There he switched to left-back, but still claimed an impressive 16 assists and eight goals.

Lewis O'Brien **28**

POSITION: Midfielder **COUNTRY:** England **DOB:** 14/10/1998

Dynamic midfielder terrier Lewis has added bite and experience to the Boro midfield mix after arriving just before the deadline on loan from Nottingham Forest. He played 100 games for Huddersfield and helped them reach the Play-Off final then switched to Forest in the Premier League and also had a spell on loan to MLS side DC United under England legend Wayne Rooney.

SQUAD

2023/24

Sam Greenwood — 29

POSITION: **Midfielder**   COUNTRY: **England**   DOB: **26/01/2002**

Versatile Sam can play anywhere in midfield, on either wing and as a striker. Having come through Arsenal's Academy he moved to Leeds. He played 18 Premier League games last season for United and had a host of clubs chasing him before opting for a loan switch to Boro. He has played at every level for England up to Under-21.

Jamie Jones — 32

POSITION: **Goalkeeper**   COUNTRY: **England**   DOB: **18/02/1989**

Experienced shot-stopper Jamie arrived at Boro in the summer to add competition and knowhow in the keeper camp. He has played over 400 senior games in a lengthy career that has included spells as number one at Leyton Orient, Preston North End and Wigan, where he won the League One title.

SHOOTING FROM DISTANCE

Good service is obviously important, and a good understanding with your striking partner is also vital, but when it comes to spectacular strikes, practice is the key to hitting a consistently accurate and powerful shot and to developing the timing and power required.

EXERCISE

A small-sided pitch is set up with two 18-yard boxes put together, but the corners of the pitch are cut off as shown in the diagram. There are five players per team, including goalkeepers, but only one player is allowed in the opponent's half.

The aim of the drill is to work a shooting opportunity when you have the ball, with the likely chance being to shoot from outside your opponent's penalty area, from distance. The teams take it in turns to release the ball into play from their own 'keeper - usually by rolling out to an unmarked player.

18 YDS

KEY FACTORS

1. **Attitude to shooting - be positive, have a go!**
2. **Technique - use laces, hit through the ball.**
3. **Do not sacrifice accuracy for power.**
4. **Wide angle shooting - aim for the far post.**
5. **Always follow up for rebounds!**

SOCCER SKILLS

The size of the pitch can be reduced for younger players, and it should be noted that these junior players should also be practicing with a size 4 or even a size 3 ball, depending on their age.

8 RILEY McGREE

23

MIDDLESBROUGH FC
WOMEN

In May 2023, Boro Women were welcomed as part of Middlesbrough FC.

On the back of the official affiliation, Boro's Chief Executive Neil Bausor said: "It's no secret that the affiliation of an MFC women's team has been under discussion for a period of time, and we now believe the infrastructure is in place to move forward.

"The club is wholly committed in its backing of MFC Women and we are excited about the future."

As part of the Boro family, the women's team now wear our crest and kit, train at Rockliffe Park, and play some games at the Riverside Stadium as well as regular venue Stockton Town.

Boro Women had enjoyed some success last season, coming from behind to beat Redcar Town 3-2 in the North Riding County FA Women's cup final.

Michael Mulhern - who has previously worked with England stars like Jill Scott, Steph Houghton, Lucy Bronze and Beth Mead - was also appointed head coach as part of the merger, and made a dozen new signings over the summer as he put his stamp on the team.

This season, Boro Women are competing in the FA Women's National League Division One North, alongside the likes of Hull City, Leeds United, Durham Cestria and York City.

Just hours after the England Lionesses faced Spain in the final of the women's World Cup in August, Boro Women kicked off their own new era with the first match of the season, a goalless draw against Norton & Stockton Ancients.

As this annual went to print, Mulhern and his team were preparing for a momentous first match for the team at the Riverside, against Stockport County.

DAZZLING DEFENDERS

TONY MOWBRAY, GARY PALLISTER AND GIANLUCA FESTA WERE ALL OUTSTANDING MIDDLESBROUGH DEFENDERS AND CONTINUING THAT TRADITION IS CURRENT CENTRE-BACK DARRAGH LENIHAN.

Although he was born in Kent, Gary Pallister grew up in County Durham and was a Middlesbrough fan as a kid. Spotted by Boro playing for non-league Billingham Town, the central-defender signed for his boyhood club in 1984 at the age of 19.

He quickly became a regular in Boro's backline, playing in 156 league matches in nearly five seasons prior to a transfer to Manchester United in August 1989.

After winning 15 trophies at Old Trafford, 'Pally' returned to Middlesbrough in July 1998 at the age of 33 and went on to feature in a further 61 matches for the club in all competitions before retiring in July 2001.

Known by the Boro faithful as 'Mogga', local lad Tony Mowbray made his debut for the club in 1982 and was appointed club captain in 1986 at the age of just 22.

He played all 46 league matches for Boro in 1986/87 as he skippered the club to the runners-up spot in the Third Division and promotion. He was an ever-present once again the following season as Boro finished third in the Second Division to regain their place in the top flight of English football.

Mowbray departed for Celtic part of the way through the 1991/92 season - another promotion-winning campaign for Middlesbrough. He returned to manage the club between 2010 and 2013.

TONY MOWBRAY

DATE OF BIRTH: November 22, 1963

PLACE OF BIRTH: Saltburn, North Yorkshire

NATIONALITY: English

BORO APPEARANCES: 424

BORO GOALS: 30

BORO DEBUT: September 8, 1982
Newcastle United 1-1 Middlesbrough (Second Division)

GARY PALLISTER

DATE OF BIRTH: June 30, 1965

PLACE OF BIRTH: Ramsgate, Kent

NATIONALITY: English

BORO APPEARANCES: 250

BORO GOALS: 7

BORO DEBUT: August 17, 1985
Wimbledon 3-0 Middlesbrough (Second Division)

Gianluca Festa immediately endeared himself to the Riverside Stadium faithful when he scored on his Boro debut in a 4-2 win over Sheffield Wednesday in January 1997 following a move from Inter Milan.

Festa was on target in the 1997 FA Cup semi-final with an effort against Chesterfield that helped take Boro to Wembley. He netted in that year's final, but his 'goal' was ruled out for offside.

He was named the club's Player of the Year in 1998 as he helped Boro gain instant promotion back to the Premier League following relegation the previous season.

GIANLUCA FESTA

DATE OF BIRTH:	March 15, 1969
PLACE OF BIRTH:	Cagliari, Italy
NATIONALITY:	Italian
BORO APPEARANCES:	171
BORO GOALS:	12
BORO DEBUT:	January 18, 1997

Middlesbrough 4-2 Sheffield Wednesday (Premier League)

DARRAGH LENIHAN

DATE OF BIRTH:	March 16, 1994
PLACE OF BIRTH:	Dunboyne, Republic of Ireland
NATIONALITY:	Irish
BORO APPEARANCES:	43*
BORO GOALS:	0*
BORO DEBUT:	July 30, 2022

Middlesbrough 1-1 West Bromwich Albion (Championship)

*AS AT THE END OF THE 2022/23 SEASON

Republic of Ireland international defender Darragh Lenihan enjoyed an exceptional debut campaign at the Riverside Stadium following a move from Blackburn Rovers in June 2022.

The 29-year-old featured in 41 of Boro's 46 Championship fixtures in 2022/23 as the club secured fourth spot at the end of the season. The Dunboyne-born player made his senior international debut against the United States in June 2018 - one of four caps to his name at the time of writing.

One of the first names on Head Coach Michael Carrick's team sheet, Lenihan started the first four matches in all competitions in 2023/24 prior to this Annual being printed.

EMMANUEL
LATTE LATH

FOOTY
PHRASES

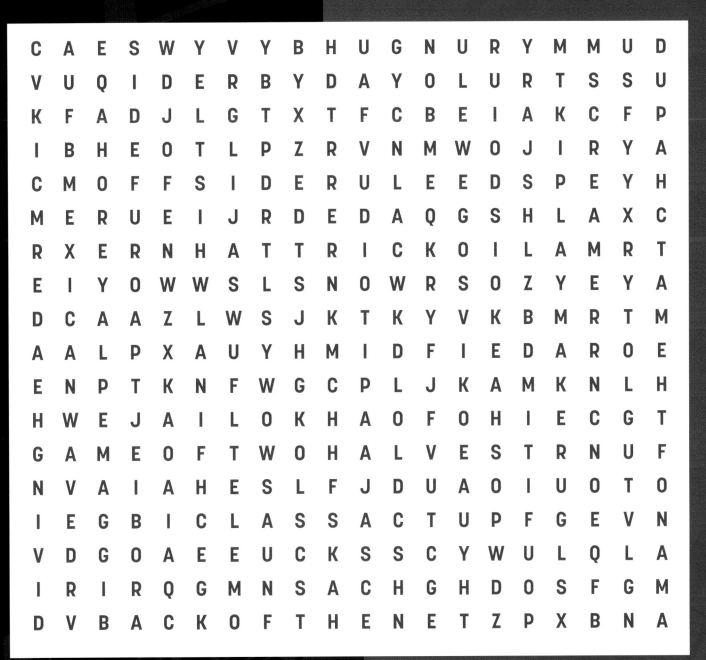

```
C A E S W Y V V B H U G N U R Y M M U D
V U Q I D E R B Y D A Y O L U R T S S U
K F A D J L G T X T F C B E I A K C F P
I B H E O T L P Z R V N M W O J I R Y A
C M O F F S I D E R U L E E D S P E Y H
M E R U E I J R D E D A Q G S H L A X C
R X E R N H A T T R I C K O I L A M R T
E I Y O W W S L S N O W R S O Z Y E Y A
D C A A Z L W S J K T K Y V K B M R T M
A A L P X A U Y H M I D F I E D A R O E
E N P T K N F W G C P L J K A M K N L H
H W E J A I L O K H A O F O H I E C G T
G A M E O F T W O H A L V E S T R N U F
N V A I A H E S L F J D U A O I U O T O
I E G B I C L A S S A C T U P F G E V N
V D G O A E E U C K S S C Y W U L Q L A
I R I R Q G M N S A C H G H D O S F G M
D V B A C K O F T H E N E T Z P X B N A
```

Back of the Net

Big Game Player

Brace

Class Act

Derby Day

Diving Header

Dugout

Dummy Run

Final Whistle

Game of Two Halves

Half Volley

Hat-trick

Keepie Uppie

Man of the Match

Mexican Wave

Offside Rule

One-touch

Playmaker

Scissor Kick

Screamer

PLAYER
OF THE SEASON

Chuba Akpom crowned a memorable season on Teesside in 2022/23 by securing a clean sweep of Player of the Season awards, as he was voted by his teammates and fans alike.

The 27-year-old forward netted 28 league goals in 38 appearances for Boro, making him a clear choice for the club's Player of the Season awards. He also saw off competition from Coventry City's Viktor Gyökeres and Burnley's Josh Brownhill to claim the Sky Bet Championship Player of Year award.

Akpom flourished under Head Coach Michael Carrick, who was appointed in October 2022. His goals were pivotal in propelling the club to a fourth-place finish in the Championship table and a spot in the Play-Offs.

During a season of personal achievement for the Arsenal academy graduate, he achieved a historic milestone by becoming the first player in over 30 years to score 20 league goals in a single season for the club. Additionally, he etched his name in Middlesbrough folklore by scoring the 1,000th goal at the Riverside Stadium during a 1-1 draw with Stoke City in March 2023.

Akpom commented at the end of the campaign:

"It means a lot to get acknowledged for the work during the season and I'm really grateful for it. There are a lot of quality players in this league so for me to even be on the shortlist was an amazing accomplishment."

"To win it is like 'wow.' It's a massive achievement and it's amazing."

YOUNG PLAYER
OF THE SEASON

Boyhood Middlesbrough fan Hayden Hackney demonstrated ability beyond his years as he earned the title of Young Player of the Season after an excellent breakthrough campaign in 2022/23.

Throughout the season, the academy graduate made 32 appearances in all competitions for the club, yet never looked out of place at the heart of a promotion-chasing side.

The 21-year-old central midfielder signed a deal with the club in 2023 which will keep him at the club until 2027.

HAYDEN HACKNEY

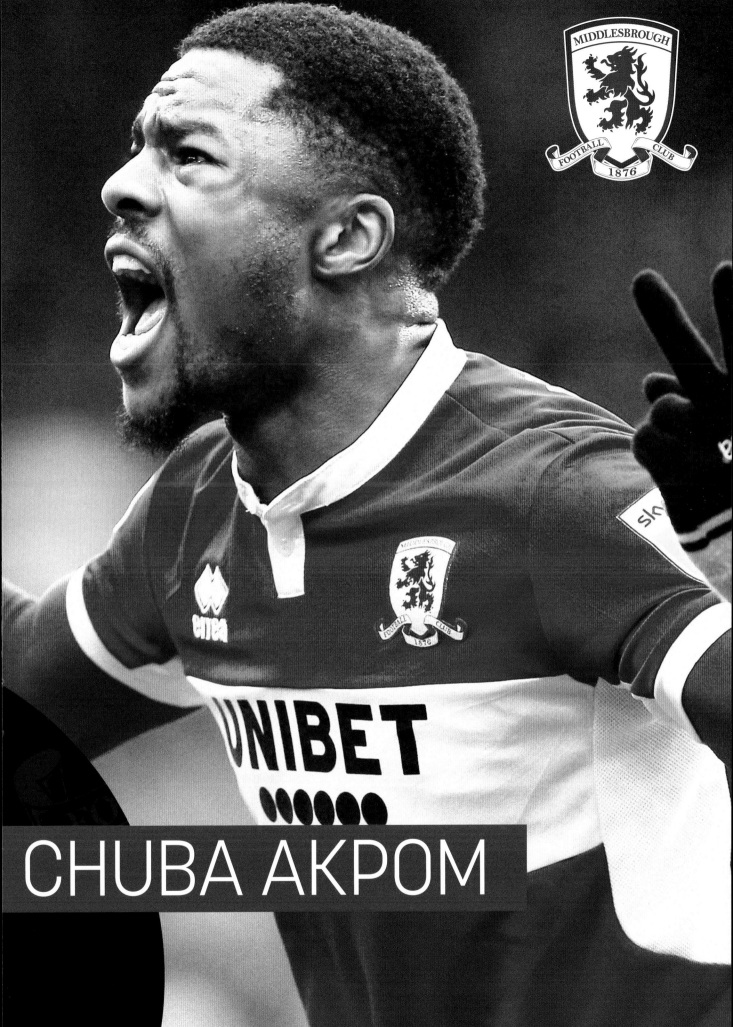

CHUBA AKPOM

THE WALL PASS

With teams being very organised in modern football, it can be very difficult to break them down and create scoring opportunities. One of the best ways to achieve this is by using the 'wall pass', otherwise known as the quick one-two.

EXERCISE

In a non-pressurised situation, involving four players, A carries the ball forward towards a static defender (in this case a cone) and before reaching the defender, plays the ball to B before running around the opposite side to receive the one-touch return pass. A then delivers the ball safely to C who then repeats the exercise returning the ball to D, and in this way the exercise continues. Eventually a defender can be used to make the exercise more challenging, with all players being rotated every few minutes.

The exercise can progress into a five-a-side game, the diagram below shows how additional players (W) on the touchline can be used as 'walls' with just one touch available to help the man in possession of the ball.

Each touchline player can move up and down the touchline, but not enter the pitch - they can also play for either team.

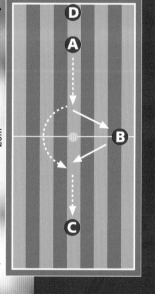

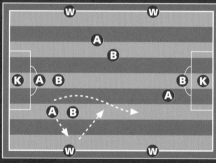

KEY FACTORS

1. Look to commit the defender before passing - do not play the ball too early.
2. Pass the ball firmly and to feet.
3. Accelerate past defender after passing.
4. Receiver (B) make themselves available for the pass.
5. B delivers a return pass, weighted correctly, into space.

SOCCER SKILLS

If done correctly, this is a tactic which is extremely difficult to stop, but needs teamwork and communication between the two attacking players.

JOSH
COBURN

A-Z

ARE YOU READY TO TACKLE OUR A-Z FOOTBALL QUIZ?

THE SIMPLE RULE IS THAT THE ANSWERS RUN THROUGH THE 26 LETTERS OF THE ALPHABET.

A
What nationality is Watford goalkeeper Daniel Bachmann?

A

B
Which team won the Sky Bet Championship title in 2022/23?

B

C
Which Premier League club reappointed their former manager as interim boss in March 2023?

C

D
Which League One side play their home matches at Pride Park?

D

E
What nationality is Liverpool's sensational striker Mohamed Salah?

E

F
Which country knocked England out of the FIFA World Cup finals in 2022?

F

G

Which famous football ground is due to host its final fixture in 2024?

G

H
Which club did Neil Warnock lead to Championship survival in 2022/23?

H

I
Which country did England defeat 6-2 in their opening game of the FIFA 2022 World Cup finals?

I

J
Aston Villa winger Leon Bailey plays internationally for which country?

J

K
What is the name of Premier League new boys Luton Town's home ground?

K

L
Can you name the Ipswich Town striker who netted 17 League One goals in the Tractor Boys' 2022/23 promotion-winning season?

L

M
Which Championship club boasted the division's top scorer in 2022/23?

M

ANSWERS ON PAGE 62

N

What nationality is Manchester City's ace marksman Erling Haaland?

N

O

Can you name the former Premier League team that will compete in the National League in 2023/24?

O

P

Which international striker ended five seasons with Norwich City in May 2023?

P

Q

Can you name the country that hosted the FIFA 2022 World Cup finals?

Q

R

Which Spanish side did Manchester City defeat in last season's UEFA Champions League semi-final?

R

S

Which team knocked Premier League champions Manchester City out of the Carabao Cup last season?

S

T

Which full-back left Huddersfield Town to join Nottingham Forest ahead of their return to the Premier League in the summer of 2022?

T

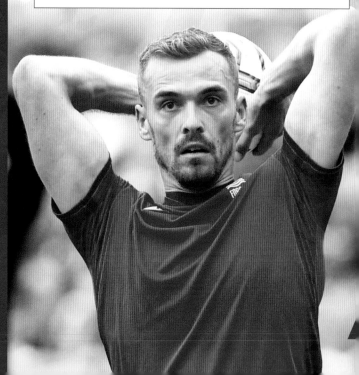

X Can you name the Portuguese international defender who played in the Premier League with Everton, Liverpool & Middlesbrough?

X

U **Can you name Brighton's German forward who joined the Seagulls in January 2022?**

U

Y At which club did Leeds United's Luke Ayling make his league debut?

Y

V Can you name the former England striker who has hit over 100 Premier League goals for Leicester City?

V

Z **Which Dutch international midfielder played Premier League football for Chelsea, Middlesbrough and Liverpool in the 2000s?**

Z

W Can you name the goalkeeper, other than Sony Dieng, who got his name on the scoresheet last season in a Championship game?

W

A-Z

PART TWO

MARCUS FORSS

21

DESIGN A FOOTY BOOT

Design a brilliant new footy boot for the Boro squad!

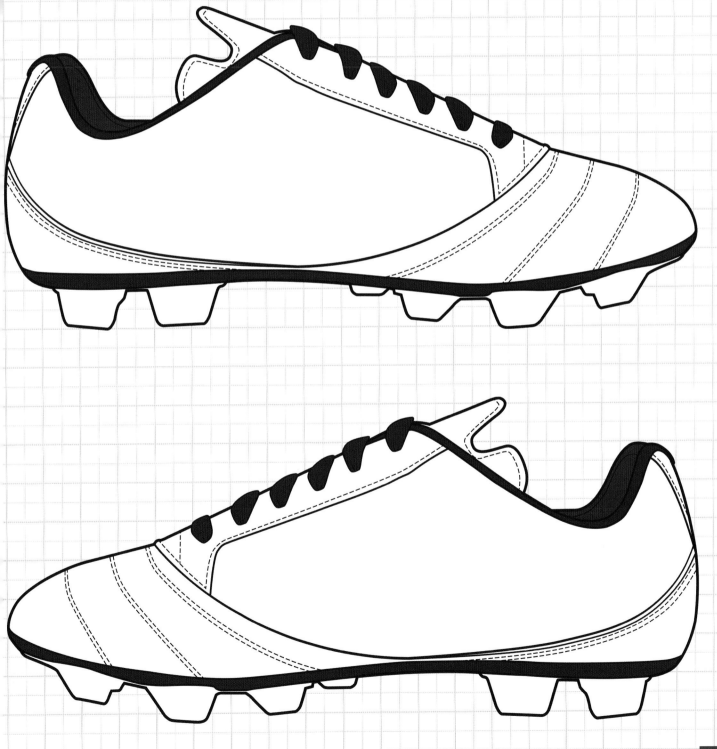

MIDFIELD
MAESTROS

GRAEME SOUNESS, JUNINHO AND STEWART DOWNING WERE ALL ENERGETIC, ALL-ACTION MIDFIELDERS FOR BORO AND CONTINUING THAT FINE TRADITION IS AUSTRALIA INTERNATIONAL, RILEY McGREE.

Born Osvaldo Giroldo Júnior, Juninho's affection for Middlesbrough was such that he played for the club in three separate spells.

He originally signed from São Paulo FC for a reported fee of £4.75m in October 1995 and, on his debut against Leeds United the following month, he made an assist for Jan Åge Fjørtoft to score. The Brazilian netted 17 goals in 69 matches in his first spell at the Riverside, but departed for Atlético Madrid in the summer of 1997 following Boro's relegation.

He returned on a season-long loan in 1999/2000 then re-signed permanently in 2002, winning the Football League Cup with the club two years later.

Graeme Souness' exploits as a player at Liverpool are well-known, with the former Scotland international having claimed five league titles, four Football League Cups and three European Cups during his time at Anfield between 1978 and 1984.

Having only made one substitute appearance for Tottenham Hotspur at the start of his senior career, it was his time at Middlesbrough that really propelled him to the legendary player he would become.

The midfielder played over 200 games for Boro between 1972 and 1978 and helped the club to Second Division title glory in 1973/74 as he scored seven goals in 35 league matches that season.

GRAEME SOUNESS

DATE OF BIRTH:	May 6, 1953
PLACE OF BIRTH:	Edinburgh, Scotland
NATIONALITY:	Scottish
BORO APPEARANCES:	216
BORO GOALS:	27
BORO DEBUT:	January 6, 1973
Fulham 2-1 Middlesbrough (Second Division)	

JUNINHO

DATE OF BIRTH:	February 22, 1973
PLACE OF BIRTH:	São Paulo, Brazil
NATIONALITY:	Brazilian
BORO APPEARANCES:	155
BORO GOALS:	34
BORO DEBUT:	November 4, 1995
Middlesbrough 1-1 Leeds United (Premier League)	

Having risen through the ranks at the Riverside Stadium, Stewart Downing scored 22 goals in 234 appearances in his first eight seasons in the club's first team prior to a 2009 transfer to Aston Villa.

During his first spell with Boro, he won the Football League Cup in 2004 and helped the club reach the 2006 UEFA Cup Final. Returning to the Riverside from West Ham United in 2015, Downing scored three goals in 45 Championship matches in 2015/16 as Boro gained promotion back to the Premier League.

He left for Blackburn Rovers in 2019, where he retired in 2021 having won 35 caps for England during his career.

STEWART DOWNING

DATE OF BIRTH: July 22, 1984

PLACE OF BIRTH: Middlesbrough

NATIONALITY: English

BORO APPEARANCES: 404

BORO GOALS: 33

BORO DEBUT: April 24, 2002
Ipswich Town 1-1 Middlesbrough (Premier League)

RILEY McGREE

DATE OF BIRTH: November 2, 1998

PLACE OF BIRTH: Gawler, Australia

NATIONALITY: Australian

BORO APPEARANCES: 57*

BORO GOALS: 8*

BORO DEBUT: February 12, 2022
Middlesbrough 4-1 Derby County (Championship)

*AS AT THE END OF THE 2022/23 SEASON

Australia midfielder Riley McGree joined Middlesbrough from MLS side Charlotte FC in January 2022.

In his first full season with Boro in 2022/23, he weighed in with six goals in 43 matches and bagged the winner in the Wear-Tees derby victory over Sunderland in September 2022. Boro went on to reach the Championship Play-Offs at the end of the 2022/23 season.

He was part of the Socceroos' 2022 FIFA World Cup squad in Qatar where he started all of his country's four matches, playing against eventual champions Argentina and runners-up France in the process.

CLASSIC

Roary is hiding in the crowd in five different places as Boro fans celebrate winning promotion to the Premier League at Molineux in 1992.

FAN'TASTIC

Can you find all five?

ANSWERS ON PAGE 62

ISAIAH

JONES

11

10

MORGAN
ROGERS

GOAL

OF THE SEASON

In November 2022, Australian international midfielder Riley McGree produced a stunning strike against Norwich City that secured him Boro's 2022/23 Goal of Season award.

In the 64th minute of a closely fought match at Carrow Road, Norwich defender Sam McCallum cleared the ball, sending it just shy of the centre circle. The dropping ball was met by the head of Boro skipper Jonny Howson, who knocked it towards Finnish striker Marcus Forss.

Suddenly, McGree surged forward from midfield, capitalising on Forss's clever header, and unleashed a breath-taking left-footed volley that found the top right corner of Angus Gunn's net. The goal instantly silenced the home crowd, leaving only the resounding cheers of the jubilant travelling fans echoing throughout the stadium.

The goal's extraordinary nature left a lasting impression on both the fans and the player himself, so much so that there was hardly any debate that it deserved to win the award. When later questioned about it, McGree humbly admitted,

"If you asked me to replicate it, it might take a while."

After the goal, Middlesbrough continued to maintain relentless pressure on the home side, and their persistence paid off in the 92nd minute when Matt Crooks managed to poke in the decisive winner.

In that same week the Socceroos midfielder received a call-up to Australia's 2022 FIFA World Cup squad, his strike - combined with Matt Crooks' late winner - claimed a 2-1 victory in Norfolk that meant Middlesbrough climbed to 14th in the table, leaving them just four points outside the Play-Offs.

In winning the award, McGree faced tough competition from players like Championship Player of Year Chuba Akpom, who scored a number of memorable strikes throughout the season. Akpom's double against Blackpool at the Riverside in February 2023 for example featured two goals that were both candidates for the award.

McGree's goal came soon after the appointment of Michael Carrick as the club's Head Coach and during a period of improved which ultimately resulted in Boro finishing fourth in the Championship in 2022/23.

RILEY McGREE

BEHIND THE

BADGE

...HIDDEN BEHIND OUR BEAUTIFUL BADGE?

A

B

C

48

D

F

G

E

H

HAYDEN
HACKNEY

TRUE COLOURS

HAVE FUN COLOURING IN
THIS PICTURE OF BORO STAR

HAYDEN HACKNEY

51

STUNNING STRIKERS

BERNIE SLAVEN, FABRIZIO RAVANELLI AND JOHN HICKTON WERE ALL ACE BORO MARKSMEN. LOOKING TO FOLLOW IN THEIR FOOTSTEPS IS ENGLAND U20 STAR MORGAN ROGERS.

Scotland-born, Republic of Ireland international Bernie Slaven joined Middlesbrough from Albion Rovers in 1985 for a fee of £25,000.

His 17 strikes in 46 Third Division matches in 1986/87 saw Boro gain promotion and he followed that up with 21 goals in 44 Second Division appearances in 1987/88 as the Teessiders reached the top flight. Relegated in 1989, Slaven played his part in another promotion in 1992 to the newly-established Premier League.

The first of his two strikes in a 2-0 win over Manchester City in August 1992 saw him become the first Irish player to score a Premier League goal.

John Hickton stands fourth on Middlesbrough's top, all-time goalscorers list after George Camsell, George Elliott and Brian Clough with 187 strikes for Boro.

Hickton scored a penalty in a 3-2 win over Workington on his debut for the club following a switch from Sheffield Wednesday. That was the first of 499 matches Hickton played for Boro between 1966 and 1977, placing him third on the club's list of top, all-time appearance makers after Tim Williamson and Gordon Jones.

During Hickton's time as a Boro player, the club were promoted to the Second Division in 1967 and the top flight in 1973/74 and won the Anglo-Scottish Cup in 1976.

JOHN HICKTON

DATE OF BIRTH:	September 24, 1944
PLACE OF BIRTH:	Chesterfield, Derbyshire
NATIONALITY:	English
BORO APPEARANCES:	499
BORO GOALS:	187
BORO DEBUT:	September 24, 1966 Middlesbrough 3-2 Workington (Third Division)

BERNIE SLAVEN

DATE OF BIRTH:	November 13, 1960
PLACE OF BIRTH:	Paisley, Renfrewshire, Scotland
NATIONALITY:	Scottish
BORO APPEARANCES:	381
BORO GOALS:	146
BORO DEBUT:	October 12, 1985 Leeds United 1-0 Middlesbrough (Second Division)

In the same year he won the UEFA Champions League with Juventus, Fabrizio Ravanelli joined Middlesbrough for £7m.

The 'White Feather' scored 69 goals in 159 appearances during his time at Juve, where he also won the UEFA Cup, Serie A and the Coppa Italia. Arriving with a big reputation, the Italian quickly settled into life on Teesside with a hat-trick on his Boro debut in a 3-3 draw on the opening weekend of the 1996/97 Premier League season.

After a short but sweet spell at the Riverside Stadium, which saw him net 32 times in 50 matches, he departed for Marseille in September 1997.

FABRIZIO RAVANELLI

DATE OF BIRTH:	December 11, 1968
PLACE OF BIRTH:	Perugia, Italy
NATIONALITY:	Italian
BORO APPEARANCES:	50
BORO GOALS:	32
BORO DEBUT:	August 17, 1996

Middlesbrough 3-3 Liverpool (Premier League)

MORGAN ROGERS

DATE OF BIRTH:	July 26, 2002
PLACE OF BIRTH:	Halesowen, West Midlands
NATIONALITY:	English
BORO APPEARANCES:	4*
BORO GOALS:	0*
BORO DEBUT:	April 11, 1999

Norwich City 0 Ipswich Town 0 (Nationwide Division One)

*AS OF AUGUST 20, 2023

Morgan Rogers signed for Boro from Manchester City ahead of the start of the 2023/24 season.

Aged 21 at the time, his arrival provided the Riverside Stadium faithful with a real cause for optimism, despite the departure of the 2022/23 season's leading scorer, Chuba Akpom, to Ajax that same summer.

As part of his football education with Manchester City, the 6ft 4in frontman gained valuable first-team experience with loan spells at Lincoln City, AFC Bournemouth and Blackpool before he agreed to a four-year contract with Boro in July 2023, becoming the club's fifth major signing of that summer after Alex Gilbert, Rav van den Berg, Tom Glover and Sam Silvera.

REWIND

THREE GREAT MIDDLESBROUGH VICTORIES FROM 2023

Sheffield United 1
Middlesbrough 3

SKY BET CHAMPIONSHIP · FEBRUARY 15, 2023

Boro kept the pressure on Sheffield United as they gave their hopes of automatic promotion a boost with an eye-catching 3-1 midweek win at Bramall Lane in February 2023.

Despite conceding a fifth-minute opener to Blades' striker Oli McBurnie, Michael Carrick's side swiftly worked their way back into the contest and were level before the break thanks to Chuba Akpom 25th-minute equaliser.

A second-half brace from Cameron Archer capped off a superb away performance as all three points headed back to the Riverside Stadium.

Middlesbrough 5
Reading 0

SKY BET CHAMPIONSHIP · MARCH 4, 2023

In-form Chuba Akpom riffled home another two goals as Boro thrashed struggling Reading 5-0 at the Riverside Stadium to begin March 2023 in emphatic style.

It certainly proved to be a torturous return to his former club for Reading boss Paul Ince as Akpom opened the scoring from the penalty spot on 24 minutes. On-loan Aaron Ramsey then added a second in first-half injury-time.

Akpom scored his second just three minutes after the re-start and Ramsey then made it 4-0 with his brace just three minutes later. Marcus Forss then netted the fifth goal of the afternoon when he converted a 76th-minute penalty.

Middlesbrough 3
Hull City 1

SKY BET CHAMPIONSHIP · APRIL 19, 2023

Boro followed up their 5-1 mauling of Norwich City at the Riverside Stadium with a second home win in the space of five days as Hull City were beaten 3-1.

Trailing 1-0 at the break, Michael Carrick's half-time team talk certainly had the desired effect as Boro scored three goals in a sensational six-minute spell to turn the contest around.

Goals from Hayden Hackney, Cameron Archer and a 29th of the campaign for Chuba Akpom ensured Boro were ending the season in fine form.

FAST FORWARD

...AND THREE BIG CHAMPIONSHIP ENCOUNTERS TO COME IN 2024...

Leicester City (AWAY)

SKY BET CHAMPIONSHIP · FEBRUARY 17, 2024

Something of a surprise arrival in the Championship for 2023/24 following relegation last season, Leicester City will host Boro on February 17 in what could well be one of our toughest assignments on the road this season.

Despite last season's disappointment, Leicester City have enjoyed the most successful period in the club's history in recent times with the Foxes crowned Premier League champions in 2016 and FA Cup winners in 2021.

Under new head coach Enzo Maresca, Leicester will be among the favourites for an instant return to the Premier League in 2023/24.

Southampton (AWAY)

SKY BET CHAMPIONSHIP · MARCH 29, 2024

The important month of March concludes with the long trip to the south coast for a vital Championship meeting with Southampton.

Just like Leicester City, Southampton were also relegated from the Premier League in 2022/23 and are sure to provide a tough challenge for Michael Carrick's men when they travel to St Mary's Stadium on Good Friday.

Southampton are another club who made a managerial change in the summer of 2023 with former MK Dons and Swansea City head coach Russell Martin being the man appointed to spearhead the Saints' promotion ambitions for 2023/24.

Leeds United (HOME)

SKY BET CHAMPIONSHIP · APRIL 20, 2024

Leeds United complete the trio of teams relegated from the Premier League last season and will be strongly fancied to mount a serious bid for promotion back to the top flight at the first time of asking.

The Elland Road club are now under the management of former Norwich City boss Daniel Farke. The German won the Championship title twice with the Canaries and will be going in search of a hat-trick of second tier titles in 2023/24.

Leeds United will be Boro's penultimate home opponents in the busy month of April ahead of a trip to Cardiff City and a final-day fixture against Watford at the Riverside Stadium.

TURNING
WITH
THE BALL

One of the biggest problems a defence can have to deal with is when a skilful player is prepared to turn with the ball and run at them, committing a key defender into making a challenge. Because football today is so fast and space so precious, this is becoming a rare skill.

EXERCISE 1

In an area 20m x 10m, A plays the ball into B who turns, and with two touches maximum plays the ball into C. C controls and reverses the process. After a few minutes the middleman is changed.

As you progress, a defender is brought in to oppose B, and is initially encouraged to play a 'passive' role. B has to turn and play the ball to C who is allowed to move along the baseline.

The type of turns can vary. Players should be encouraged to use the outside of the foot, inside of the foot, with feint and disguise to make space for the turn.

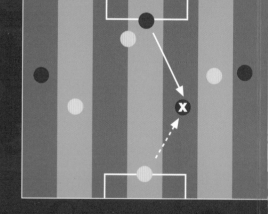

EXERCISE 2

As the players grow in confidence, you can move forward to a small-sided game. In this example of a 4-a-side practice match, X has made space for himself to turn with the ball, by coming off his defender at an angle. By doing this he can see that the defender has not tracked him, and therefore has the awareness to turn and attack.

SOCCER
SKILLS

Matches at the top level are won and lost by pieces of skill such as this, so players have to be brave enough to go in search of the ball, and turn in tight situations.

18

SAMMY
SILVERA

HIGH FIVES

TEST YOUR MIDDLESBROUGH KNOWLEDGE & MEMORY WITH OUR HIGH FIVES QUIZ

1. Across the previous five seasons, who have been Boro's leading league goalscorers?

1. _____
2. _____
3. _____
4. _____
5. _____

3. Prior to Michael Carrick, who were the club's last five permanent managers?

1. _____
2. _____
3. _____
4. _____
5. _____

2. Can you name Boro's last five FA Cup opponents ahead of the 2023/24 season?

1. _____
2. _____
3. _____
4. _____
5. _____

4. Can you name our last five EFL Cup opponents as at the end of 2022/23?

1. _____
2. _____
3. _____
4. _____
5. _____

5. Can you remember Boro's final league position from each of the last five seasons?

1. _____
2. _____
3. _____
4. _____
5. _____

8. Can you recall the score and season from our last five derby wins over Sunderland?

1. _____
2. _____
3. _____
4. _____
5. _____

6. Which members of the Middlesbrough squad started the most league games last season?

1. _____
2. _____
3. _____
4. _____
5. _____

9. Can you remember Boro's final five Championship victories from last season?

1. _____
2. _____
3. _____
4. _____
5. _____

7. Can you recall the following players' squad numbers from the 2022/23 season?

1. Dael Fry _____
2. Matt Crooks _____
3. Isaiah Jones _____
4. Marcus Forss _____
5. Jonny Howson _____

10. Name the last five players to score two or more in a match for Boro prior to 2023/24?

1. _____
2. _____
3. _____
4. _____
5. _____

SENSATIONAL STOPPERS

JIM PLATT, STEPHEN PEARS AND MARK SCHWARZER WERE ALL GREAT MIDDLESBROUGH 'KEEPERS. NEW ARRIVAL SENY DIENG WILL BE LOOKING TO CONTINUE THAT FINE TRADITION.

Stephen Pears joined Middlesbrough on loan during the 1983/84 season, during which time he made twelve league appearances.

Boro looked to secure his services on a regular basis, but were unable to afford the £80,000 fee parent club Manchester United were looking for. He eventually sealed a permanent move from Old Trafford to Ayresome Park in 1985. An excellent performer in 1985/86, despite Boro's relegation to the old Third Division, Pears was a key member of the team that achieved back-to-back promotions in 1986/87 and 1987/88 to reach the top flight.

He was released in 1995 after a sell-out testimonial match where he notched the last-ever goal at Ayresome Park from the penalty spot.

Born in Ballymoney, Northern Ireland on January 26, 1952, Jim Platt stands fifth on Middlesbrough's top, all-time appearance makers list having donned a Boro goalkeeper shirt on no less than 481 occasions between 1971 and 1983.

Platt was a key member of Jack Charlton's class of 1973/74 that won the old Second Division title and remained in the top flight with Boro for eight consecutive seasons after that.

He played in both legs of Boro's Anglo-Scottish Cup Final against Fulham in 1975, which saw the club win 1-0 on aggregate. He was capped 23 times by Northern Ireland between 1976 and 1986.

JIM PLATT

DATE OF BIRTH:	January 26, 1952
PLACE OF BIRTH:	Ballymoney, Northern Ireland
NATIONALITY:	Northern Irish
BORO APPEARANCES:	481
BORO DEBUT:	October 2, 1971

Middlesbrough 1-0 Blackpool (Second Division)

STEPHEN PEARS

DATE OF BIRTH:	January 22, 1962
PLACE OF BIRTH:	Brandon, County Durham
NATIONALITY:	English
BORO APPEARANCES:	257
BORO DEBUT:	November 5, 1983

Middlesbrough 2-0 Cardiff City (Second Division)

Australia's most capped player, with 109 appearances for the Socceroos between 1993 and 2013, Mark Schwarzer joined Boro from Bradford City in 1997.

His first silverware with the club came in the shape of the League Cup, which Boro won in 2004, while he also started in the 1997 and 1998 League Cup Finals and the 2006 UEFA Cup Final.

Schwarzer played 34 First Division matches for Middlesbrough in 1997/98 which saw the club gain promotion while he has played more Premier League matches - 332 - for Boro than anyone else. He departed for Fulham in 2008.

MARK SCHWARZER

DATE OF BIRTH:	October 6, 1972
PLACE OF BIRTH:	North Richmond, Australia
NATIONALITY:	Australian
BORO APPEARANCES:	445
BORO DEBUT:	February 26, 1997

Stockport County 0 Middlesbrough 2 (League Cup)

SENY DIENG

DATE OF BIRTH:	November 23, 1994
PLACE OF BIRTH:	Zürich, Switzerland
NATIONALITY:	Senegalese
BORO APPEARANCES:	3*
BORO DEBUT:	August 5, 2023

Middlesbrough 0 Millwall 1 (Championship)

*AS OF AUGUST 20, 2023

A proven performer at Championship level with Queens Park Rangers, for whom he made 120 appearances in all competitions between 2016 and 2023, Seny Dieng was one of three new goalkeepers to join Middlesbrough in the summer of 2023.

Boro reportedly paid £2m to secure the Senegal international's services, with the stopper putting pen-to-paper on a four-year contract at the Riverside.

Dieng made his Boro debut in the club's 2023/24 Championship opening-day fixture at home to Millwall and maintained the starting spot for a trip to Coventry City and a clash with Huddersfield Town at the Riverside Stadium early in the campaign.

ANSWERS

PAGE 29: FOOTY PHRASES
Keepie Uppie.

PAGE 34: A-Z QUIZ
A. Austrian. B. Burnley. C. Crystal Palace. D. Derby County. E. Egyptian. F. France. G. Goodison Park (Everton). H. Huddersfield Town. I. Iran. J. Jamaica. K. Kenilworth Road. L. Ladapo, Freddie. M. Middlesbrough (Chuba Akpom). N. Norwegian. O. Oldham Athletic. P. Pukki, Teemu. Q. Qatar. R. Real Madrid. S. Southampton. T. Toffolo, Harry. U. Undav, Deniz. V. Vardy, Jamie. W. Wilson, Ben (Coventry City). X. Xavier, Abel. Y. Yeovil Town. Z. Zenden, Boudewijn.

PAGE 42: FAN'TASTIC

PAGE 48: BEHIND THE BADGE
A. Daniel Barlaser. B. Morgan Rogers. C. Hayden Coulson. D. Hayden Hackney. E. Matt Crooks. F. Jonny Howson. G. Darragh Lenihan. H. Sammy Silvera.

PAGE 58: HIGH FIVES
QUIZ 1:
1. 2022/23, Chuba Akpom (28 goals).
2. 2021/22, Matt Crooks (10 goals).
3. 2020/21 Duncan Watmore (9 goals).
4. 2019/20, Britt Assombalonga and Ashley Fletcher (11 goals each).
5. 2018/19, Britt Assombalonga (14 goals).

QUIZ 2:
1. 2022/23, Brighton & HA (third round).
2. 2021/22, Chelsea (quarter-final).
3. 2021/22, Tottenham Hotspur (fifth round).
4. 2021/22, Manchester United (fourth round).
5. 2021/22, Mansfield Town (third round).

QUIZ 3:
1. Chris Wilder. 2. Neil Warnock. 3. Jonathan Woodgate. 4. Tony Pulis. 5. Garry Monk.

QUIZ 4:
1. Barnsley (2022/23). 2. Blackpool (2021/22). 3. Barnsley (2020/21). 4. Shrewsbury Town (2020/21). 5. Crewe Alexandra (2019/20).

QUIZ 5:
1. 4th in Championship (2022/23). 2. 7th in Championship (2021/22). 3. 10th in Championship (2020/21). 4. 17th Championship (2019/20). 5. 7th in Championship (2018/19).

QUIZ 6:
1. Jonny Howson (44 Championship starts). 2. Ryan Giles (43 Championship starts). 3. Zack Steffen (42 Championship starts). 4. Darragh Lenihan (40 Championship starts). 5. Chuba Akpom and Riley McGree (both had 35 Championship starts).

QUIZ 7:
1. 6. 2. 25. 3. 2. 4. 21. 5. 16.

QUIZ 8:
1. 2022/23, Middlesbrough 1-0 Sunderland (Championship).
2. 2017/18, Middlesbrough 2-0 Sunderland (FA Cup).
3. 2017/18, Middlesbrough 1-0 Sunderland (Championship).
4. 2016/17, Middlesbrough 1-0 Sunderland (Premier League).
5. 2016/17, Sunderland 1-2 Middlesbrough (Premier League).

QUIZ 9:
1. Middlesbrough 3 Hull City 1. 2. Middlesbrough 5-1 Norwich City.
3. Middlesbrough 4-0 Preston NE. 4. Swansea City 1-3 Middlesbrough.
5. Middlesbrough 5-0 Reading.

QUIZ 10:
1. Cameron Archer (two v Norwich City, April 2023).
2. Cameron Archer (two v Preston North End, March 2023).
3. Chuba Akpom (two v Reading, March 2023).
4. Aaron Ramsey (two v Reading, March 2023).
5. Chuba Akpom (two v Queens Park Rangers, February 2023).